An Other Side Christmas

By O'Jay Barr

Above the
BARR PUBLISHING

Dear Reader,

While this novella features characters from The Other Side series, it also stands on its own. So, whether you've been rocking with the twins and their crew since The Other Side: Secrets, or you're just meeting them for the first time, Welcome.

This story is a little softer and a whole lot warmer. It's a chance to pause with these women, tucked away in a snowy cabin, as they navigate love, laughter, and a little bit of healing during the holidays.

And if you loved this story and want more of Samantha, Josephine, Erica, and Rose, then visit my website at www.authorojaybarr.com to purchase the full series.

Happy Holidays!

DECEMBER 22ND
JOSEPHINE

"Sam hasn't asked any questions about the trip we have planned?"

"Nope. Not a single word. Probably because I haven't told her about it yet," Rose said with a laugh.

"Wait, what?" I laughed too, confused.

"Come on. Have you ever tried surprising your sister with anything? She'll ask so many damn questions you either give up or decide it ain't even worth it anymore."

I shook my head, grinning. "You right about that. She's been like that since we were kids. She used to go hunting for Christmas and birthday gifts. Tore through every closet in the house until our parents stopped hiding them at home altogether. And the worst part? She'd ruin the surprise for me, too. Wouldn't even let me have the moment. Just came in like, 'Guess what you're getting!' That's probably why I don't really like surprises now."

"Damn, I didn't know she was that bad."

"She was. And now she's your problem," I said, raising an eyebrow.

Rose laughed again. "Exactly why I haven't told her we're going to the cabin. As far as she knows, I'm working on Christmas Day. She has no idea we're going with y'all and I wasn't about to risk her ruining the surprise for Erica either."

"The things we do for these women," I sighed dramatically. "Well, your woman.

Mine's chill. I told her I was taking her away for Christmas since her parents are going on a cruise, and she just said, 'Cool, let me know what to pack.'"

"Why can't Samantha be that easy?!"

"Sorry, bruh."

"No you're not," Rose said, laughing.

"You right," I grinned. "That just means I don't have to deal with it. I love my twin, but she's been a brat for 33 years. I'm glad somebody else gotta deal with her now."

"Anyway, we're still riding to the airport together, right? I'm packing her bags tomorrow while she's at work. Soon as she gets home, I'll tell her we're leaving. She thinks we're having dinner with you guys before your flight."

"Yep. I'll have the driver scoop y'all on the way, should be around 3:30."

"Perfect. She should be walking in any minute now. I'll holla at you later."

"Aight, peace."

I was so excited about this Christmas trip to Colorado, I could hardly sit still. When Erica told me her parents were taking a last-minute cruise and wouldn't be home for the holidays, I could see how disappointed she was. And I knew I had to do something special for my baby.

Then I remembered she's never seen snow before.

That sealed it. Cozy cabin in Colorado, just the two of us… well, four of us. I'm glad Rose and Sam are coming too. Our little family. I smiled at the thought.

I really wanted to visit Charlie, but with the twins being so new, we all agreed it wasn't the best time to be around them. Covid's still lurking, and I wasn't about to put her or the babies at risk. For now, I'll settle for pictures and video calls until I can kiss my twin nephews in person.

I twiddled my fingers on my desk, practically vibrating with excitement, before I realized I wasn't getting another damn thing done today. I shut down my computer, grabbed my keys and wallet, and dipped out of the office.

Erica was cooking dinner tonight, so I made a quick stop at the store on the way home and grabbed a bottle of her favorite wine. When I got to the house, I chopped up the veggies and seasoned the meat for Erica. Then I kicked off my shoes and flopped onto the couch, flipping between streaming services for something to watch while texting the chef to finalize our meals for the trip. Everything was coming together.

"Hey, baby! Let me change out of these clothes and I'll start dinner," Erica said, giving me a big kiss and a warm hug before dropping her work bag by the stairs.

"Take your time, love. I already prepped everything for you," I said, pulling her onto my lap for a longer greeting.

"You didn't have to do that, it's my night to cook." She rolled her eyes at me, but the little smile playing on her lips said she appreciated it.

"I know, but I got off early and figured I'd make myself useful. I also picked up a bottle of your favorite wine on the way home."

"Thank you, baby," she said, giving me another kiss before heading into the kitchen. A second later, she doubled back to grab her phone off the table. "Hey, girl!" she answered, already halfway up the stairs.

I smirked. That had to be Sam, probably asking her 50/11 follow-up questions about this 'quiet Christmas' we supposedly had planned. I settled into the couch after settling on watching the football game and finishing up my text thread with the chef. I wanted to make sure she had the full grocery list for the meals we'd be cooking and the menu for the ones she'd be preparing. I wasn't playing about this trip, it was going to be perfect.

A few minutes later, Erica came back down in her usual cozy-around-the-house gear: shorts and a fitted tee.

"No need to repeat that, I heard her loud and clear," she said, shaking her head. "And unfortunately, she's right. You are the worst at keeping secrets. Not-uh! I know I'm good with secrets," she called out toward me, poking her head out of the kitchen. "Right, baby?!"

"Right, baby," I said absentmindedly, barely looking up as I triple-checked the flight confirmations, cabin check-in, and the car service for both here and Colorado.

"See! Thank you, babe. Sam's trippin'. You're right, you never told any of my important secrets." Erica laughed, then added, "But you do suck at surprises, though. Yeah, I was lowkey sad about not spending Christmas together this year, too. With my parents off on their cruise, I really wanted our own little family holiday."

She came over and handed me a glass of wine. I smiled at her, but I really was smiling because I knew just how happy she was about to be. She had no idea what was coming.

She stayed on the phone with Sam for a few more minutes, nodding along and giving all the right noises to whatever dramatic tale Sam was spinning about Rose having to work Christmas morning.

"Okay, babes, we're about to have dinner. I'll see you tomorrow!" she said as she ended the call and placed two plates of chicken stir-fry with basmati rice on the table. She went back to the kitchen for her wine and the bottle.

"You find something to watch?" she asked, settling into her seat.

"Yeah, that Christmas movie you like with Kelly Rowland."

Erica grinned like a little kid. We ate and caught up on our day, then she stood to take our plates to the kitchen.

"I got it," I said, standing to help, "why don't you go shower while I clean the kitchen?"

"Thanks, baby. Plus, I need to throw a few more things in my suitcase, and then I'll be back down so we can watch Ms. Kelly find her man." She giggled as she turned toward the stairs.

"Woman, how much more can you fit in that suitcase?" I asked, crossing my arms.

"Aht aht!" she said, spinning back toward me. "You don't complain when you get to see me in all the sexy things, so don't complain when I pack all the sexy things."

"Okay, okay," I said, holding my hands up in surrender as she walked away.

I turned on some music and cleaned up the kitchen, then settled on the couch to finish the game while I waited on her. Time passed, the game went off, and she still hadn't come back. I climbed the stairs and found her knocked out across the bed, snoring lightly, with tank tops and panties tossed everywhere and her suitcase still half-open in front of the closet.

I shook my head, chuckling softly as I gathered her clothes and placed them on the chair. Then I slid into bed behind her, pulling her close.

"Your sexy things are all over the bed," I whispered against her neck, brushing a kiss over her skin as I got comfortable.

She surprised me by whispering back, "that's because I stopped packing when I realized I'm the sexy thing."

"Mmm, you absolutely are," I murmured, grinning as she giggled.

I rolled onto my back and pulled her on top of me, hands settling on her waist. "Now, what was that you were saying about keeping secrets?" I teased, my lips brushing her neck, one hand sliding lower to knead her ass.

"Just that I'm great at secrets," she tried to playfully pull away from me, but my right arm was wrapped around her waist, holding her tight against my body.

"So, tell me a secret." I was sucking on her earlobe, and she was breathing heavily.

"If I told you a secret, it wouldn't be a secret anymore."

"I won't tell anyone that you aren't as good at secrets as you think," my left hand pulled the strap on her tank top down so I could sink my teeth into her shoulder. Not enough to really hurt, but enough to elicit a half scream, half moan.

"You…can't…make…me…talk."

I worked my way from her shoulder to her breast.

I sucked her nipple while swirling my tongue around at the same time. The way she was squirming, I knew she was ready to tell me what she wore to school on the first day of kindergarten. But I also knew my fiancé wouldn't give in that easily. Before she could break away from my grip, I rolled us both over so that I was on top. Straddling her body, I sat up and pulled my sports bra off. I bent over as if I was going to kiss her, but instead, I grabbed both of her wrists, wrapped my sports bra around them, and placed her hands over her head.

"Are you sure about that?" I smiled devilishly.

I sat back on my knees between her legs and held her right leg on my shoulder. I kissed, nibbled, and licked from her ankle all the way up her leg and inner thigh. I realized Erica was holding her breath when I reached her center, but I couldn't give in that easily either, so I switched to her inner left thigh, kissing, nibbling, and licking all the way down to her ankle. Erica defiantly shook her head no, I smirked. I eased up her body, kissing, nibbling, and licking from one hip across her stomach to the other hip. Erica's back arched, and she squirmed some more. I was heading back to her breasts, and I didn't know how much longer she would be able to hold out. Straddling her body again, I grabbed both breasts, leaned down, and sucked both nipples into my mouth at the same time. A loud moan escaped from Erica before she could bite down on her lip to keep from screaming.

"Sounds like you're ready to talk?" I smiled in between flicking my tongue over her erect nipples. She shook her head again, only this time it looked to be more so in the midst of passion than as an answer. I took it for the latter and sucked harder.

"Dammit Jo," she cried out in ecstasy. I smirked and slid one finger inside of her. She bucked her hips up at my touch. After removing my finger, I rubbed it against her lips and into her mouth so that she could taste herself. She gasped and bit her lip simultaneously when I slid two fingers inside. I bent down and she kissed me with such heat and passion that I felt lightheaded.

"Tell me what you want me to do to you." I was back kissing her neck while rubbing her clit.

"Jo…." Her hips were rotating in sync with my movements.

"Say it…" Another bite on her shoulder.

"Please."

"Not until you tell me," I demanded.

"I want you to eat me out."

"Say please, again."

"Jo, please." She whimpered.

I was satisfied as I slid back down her body, staring her in the eyes the whole time before sucking her clit into my mouth. Erica's back arched again, and she started to move her hands so that she could grab my head.

"If you move your hands, I will start all over again." I threatened her.

What's the saying, if looks could kill? She did as she was told and put her hands back over her head. Once she was back in position, I returned my attention and my tongue to her clit. Just when I thought she couldn't take any more, I slid a finger inside her. That did it, she melted, calling my name and cursing the whole time. She tried to slide away from me, but I held her in place, licking and sucking until her orgasm was over. When I was satisfied that she was finished, I gave her one final lick and released the hold I had on her thighs. Smiling the entire time, I straddled her body and removed my sports bra from her wrists before collapsing on the bed next to her.

"You don't play fair," She whispered, trying to catch her breath.

"It was never my intention to do so."

"Oh, really? Two can play at that game, you know."

I was not expecting her to recover that quickly, so before I could respond, she was on top of me again.

"So, you think you're going to get me to talk?"

"I don't need you to talk, baby, just to moan."

I was soaking wet and ready to go. Erica slid my shorts off and buried her face between my thighs. I immediately reacted, grinding against her face and holding her head in place. I don't even know if she could breathe, but damn, I loved it. I could feel my juices dripping down my crack as I got increasingly excited and closer to my orgasm. She sucked my clit in her mouth and swirled her tongue around it, sending me through the roof. I clutched the sheets and tightened my thighs around her head. When I finally released her from the vice grip of my thighs, I looked down to catch her grinning.

"Get up here," I ordered. She wiped her mouth and chin, still cheesing, and crawled slowly up my body. "I hate when you do that." I scowled and kissed her softly.

"Do what?" Erica asked in an innocent tone.

"Make me cum in two minutes," I chuckled.

"Oh, that's my mission in life," she giggled.

"Good night, Erica," I rolled my eyes and snuggled her closer to me.

She smiled contentedly in my arms.

DECEMBER 23RD
ERICA

"Erica, let's go! The car is here!" Jo called up the stairs.

"Are you sure I don't need to bring anything?" I asked, stepping to the top in sweatpants, sneakers, and a cropped sweatshirt, my curls piled into a high ponytail.

"No, baby. I have everything you need. Just grab your coat and purse so we're not late."

"It would help if you'd just tell me what we're doing already," I muttered, rolling my eyes.

"You'll find out in less than an hour, luv," she said with that smug little grin. Jo held the door open and ushered me out, making sure to lock-up behind us.

I thanked our driver, Donna, as she opened the door to the Escalade. Jo tried to make small talk during the ride, but I was too busy messing with my purse and adjusting my ponytail for the third time.

"Babe, why you so nervous?" she asked. "I thought you liked surprises."

"I do… but I don't like long surprises," I giggled.

"Well, lucky for you, this one's almost over. In fact," she leaned closer with a smirk, "we're pulling up to the first part now."

I perked up and looked out the window. "Samantha's? Are you hiding a gift here?"

"No, woman. Slide over closer to me," she said, patting the seat. "They're coming too."

"What?!" I didn't slide; I jumped out of the truck the second I saw Samantha and Rose walking toward us.

"You knew?!" Sam and I squealed at the same time as we hugged each other tight.

"No! I didn't know you were coming! When did you find out?" I asked, laughing.

"Ladies," Rose cut in, looking a little flustered. "Can y'all please finish this conversation inside the vehicle? We've got somewhere else to be."

Donna stood there patiently while the three of us scrambled to get back in. I slid in first, then Sam, then Rose. She gave Jo a quick fist bump while Sam leaned over and kissed her on the cheek.

The car pulled off again and we immediately went back to talking, trying to piece together what was going on.

"Girl, I came home from work early, thinking we were meeting y'all for dinner before you left," Sam said, shaking her head. "Next thing I know, Rose has my bags packed and tells me we're going somewhere. I don't even know if she has everything!"

"Baby, of course I do," Rose said, calm as ever. "I know what you like. I know your essentials. Don't worry."

She kissed Sam on the cheek and, just like that, Sam melted right into her seat. A whole mess.

"Jo, we're here," Donna announced as we pulled into the airport.

"Okay, are you finally going to tell us where we're going?" I asked, giving Jo a look.

"Check your text messages. I just sent you your boarding passes."

I side-eyed her extra-ness and unlocked my phone.

"Colorado?!"

"Yes," Jo said, smiling. "None of us have ever had a white Christmas, so we thought it'd be something special to experience together."

"Surprise," Rose chimed in.

Sam shrieked, immediately pulling Rose into her arms and kissing her like she'd just won the lottery.

I turned to Jo and gave her a soft kiss. "Babe…this was really thoughtful. Thank you."

I caught Donna smiling at us through the rearview mirror as she slowed to a stop in front of the Delta terminal.

"Baby, did you pack enough warm clothes?" I turned to her.

Jo smirked. "Come on now… who's your woman?"

"You," I smiled, leaning in for another kiss.

"Exactly. I packed everything you'll need and on the slim change that I forgot something, Colorado's got stores."

Donna opened the door, helped us out and wished us a safe trip. We thanked her and headed inside the terminal to check our bags and get through security.

Once we made it to the concourse, we stopped at one of the little shops to grab a blanket, some travel pillows, and enough snacks to hold us over. I was too excited to eat anything heavy, so we made our way to the gate to wait.

An hour and a half flew by faster than I expected. Before I knew it, they were calling First Class, and we were boarding the plane. By the time the rest of the passengers got settled, we were already sipping cocktails and scrolling through movie options.

We picked a corny rom-com I'd seen before but loved anyway. Jo pretended to roll her eyes, but I caught her smiling more than once.

Halfway through the flight, I put my head on her shoulder and put her hand between my thighs. Taking her cue from me, she slid her hand inside my sweatpants and underwear to find me already moist. She slipped two fingers inside of me, causing me to gasp slightly. She slowly worked her fingers in and out until I was moving my hips upwards to meet her thrust. After a few minutes of this pattern, I turned my head and bit down on Jo's shoulder to keep from crying out loud.

"That's it, cum for me baby," she whispered to me, I grabbed her hand, holding it in place and tried to control my orgasmic spasms.

"Dammit Jo." I whispered back before dozing off with my head on her shoulder.

I must've dozed for a while, because the next thing I heard was someone saying, "Hey Ms. Riley. You doing okay?"

I opened one eye to see the flight attendant crouched beside Jo's seat, smiling a little too warmly.

"I'm good," Jo said, smooth and unbothered.

"Can I get you another drink?"

"Yeah. I'll take another Sky Breeze, thanks."

The attendant glanced at me. "Would your… friend like anything?"

Jo raised an eyebrow and smiled. "She's good for now. But I'll be sure to order for my fiancé when she wakes up."

The girl's whole body jolted like she forgot how legs work. "Of course! I'll be right back with that."

She stood up a little too fast and wobbled just slightly in her heels.

"Be careful now," I said with a sleepy smile, stretching. "I'd hate to see you fall."

She gave me a tight-lipped smile before disappearing behind the curtain.

A few minutes later, the male flight attendant returned with Jo's drink.

Jo took a sip and smirked. I nudged her, smiling. "Why you do that lady like that?"

She grinned. "I didn't do anything. I just made sure she knew I was off the market.

You going back to sleep?" Jo asked as I stretched just a little against her shoulder.

"Nah, I think I need to stay up and keep an eye on you."

"Me?" she shrugged innocently. "What I do?"

I glanced across the aisle, Rose and Sam were both knocked out. Completely curled into each other, not a care in the world.

We made it through two episodes of Girlfriends just as the plane began to descend. Once we landed, we grabbed our luggage and headed outside to meet our driver, only to be immediately slapped in the face by the cold. This was definitely not Atlanta cold.

Even though the driver was parked right outside the terminal door, those 15 seconds of walking felt like a whole arctic expedition. We were all shivering.

The ride to the cabin was only about thirty minutes, but the scenery? Stunning. None of us had ever seen this much snow before. Everything was covered in soft, powdery white, the trees looked like something out of a snow globe, and the sky had that dreamy winter hue that made it feel like magic.

"Oh my gosh, Jo! It looks like a winter wonderland!" Sam gasped as the cabin came into view. "Look at all the lights!" She was bouncing in her seat like a little kid.

"It does look kinda magical," I whispered, watching the warm glow of the cabin lights flicker through the snow-covered trees.

The driver opened the door and helped unload our bags onto the porch. "They didn't skimp on the Christmas decor!" I said, wide-eyed, once we were inside. There were garlands strung across the fireplace, twinkling lights wrapped around every beam, and a big wreath hanging above the entryway. Tinsel. Everywhere.

"I asked them to leave the tree bare so we could decorate it ourselves," Jo said, giving me a quick wink. "I knew how much you and Sam would want to do that."

We continued exploring the cabin and took our luggage into the bedrooms. We were all still buzzing from how beautiful everything was, so much so that none of us noticed the delicious smell coming from the kitchen right away.

When we did? Game over.

The chef had just finished and left everything out, perfectly timed so the food was still hot when we arrived.

"I didn't even realize I was hungry until right this second," Rose laughed, already reaching for a plate.

"Spiked apple cider or spiked hot chocolate?" I called out as I started pulling ingredients from the bar cabinet.

"Apple cider!" Sam and Jo said in unison.

We all laughed, and I got to work.

Dinner was quiet in the best way. Only broken up by the occasional "mmm" or "this is so good."

"You know the food's hittin' when nobody's talking," Sam said, standing to make a second plate.

We all laughed again, softer this time, just happy to be together.

After dinner, Sam and Jo cleaned the kitchen while I made popcorn and poured another round of drinks. Rose was in charge of finding us a Christmas movie.

"Thanks, twin," Sam said quietly as she leaned over and rested her head on Jo's shoulder for a second.

"You're welcome, twin," Jo said, kissing Sam on the forehead with a soft smile.

Those tender moments between them didn't happen often, so when they did, I took a mental screenshot. I caught myself smiling as I watched them. Peaceful, no bickering, just love. It made my life so much easier when those two were getting along. Jo tried not to put me in the middle of their arguments, bless her heart, but let's be real. I was her fiancé and Sam's best friend. Whether I wanted to be or not, I was always going to be in it somehow, even if it was just listening to them vent. I appreciated that Jo never expected me to pick sides…even though she always thought she was right.

"Y'all coming? Best Man Holiday isn't gonna watch itself!" Rose called from the living room.

"Yeah, come on, you two!" I teased. "Y'all getting soft on me?"

"Never!" they replied in unison, both laughing as they loaded the last dish into the dishwasher.

I followed them into the living room, where Rose had everything set up like the ultimate cozy movie night: fireplace lit, movie queued, a giant pillow and blanket pallet stretched across the floor.

"I'm taking bets on who falls asleep first," Rose said, grinning.

"No need to lose that bet. It's gonna be me, luv," Sam yawned as she curled up next to her. "I might make it halfway through the movie, but between the flight, the food, and this liquor."

"Oooh, that's licka!" I laughed, tasting my drink. "I second that, friend. Soon as this cup is done, I probably will be too."

"Why don't we just head to bed then?" Jo asked, already starting to get up.

"NO!" Sam and I said in unison, making everyone laugh.

"It's something about falling asleep out here first that makes the sleep in bed hit even harder," I explained.

"Seriously?" Rose looked over at Sam, who nodded in full agreement.

Rose and Jo sighed dramatically and flopped onto the floor next to us. Sure enough, just past the halfway mark, I heard Sam snoring softly and I dozed right behind her.

Jo nudged us gently awake one by one and we all trudged silently up the stairs. When we got to our bedroom, I stripped, washed my face, and collapsed into bed. Honestly, I don't know who fell asleep first. All I know is, I hadn't felt that full, that safe, or that loved in a long time.

DECEMBER 24TH
JOSEPHINE

"Baby… baaaabbbyyyy."

I was pulled out of sleep by soft butterfly kisses on my nose and Erica whispering in that singsong voice she used when she wanted something.

"Yes, my love?" I mumbled, eyes still closed.

"It's time to wake up," she said, now kissing me softly on the lips.

"What time is it?"

"I don't know," she giggled, "but I'm sure it's time to wake up."

"Really, baby? We're on vacation. Shouldn't we be sleeping in?"

"Who can sleep in with all the snow and lights and excitement?!"

"Me," I mumbled, rolling away from her, "I can."

"Do you wanna build a snowman?" she whispered again, and I could hear the smile in her voice.

"Erica Renee..."

And then she actually started singing the song from Frozen.

"Okay, okay, I'm up," I groaned, cracking one eye open. There was no stopping this woman once she got going. "What is it you want to do?"

"Seriously? I want to build a snowman. I've never done it. And then we can have hot chocolate and breakfast and decorate the tree! Ooh and put our gifts out, and watch a couple of Christmas movies -"

"Baby," I cut in, pulling her into a hug, "we're gonna be here until after the new year. Slow down."

She laughed, finally taking a breath. "Okay… maybe a little. But let's go! There's still a lot to do today!"

Before I could protest or convince her to stay bed, she was already out from under the covers, digging through the suitcase I packed. She pulled out snow pants, boots, and layered up in a thermal and a turtleneck like she'd been waiting her whole life for this moment.

I sat there for a second, face in my hands and then slowly climbed out of bed.

"You invite Rose and Sam to come build this snowman too, or am I the only one being tortured at the crack of dawn?"

"I called Samantha. When she didn't answer, I knocked. Rose said they'd be out front as soon as she drags Sam out of bed."

"Oh, so like… an hour from now?" I snorted.

Erica rolled her eyes. "I don't know how you two can waste time sleeping when there's so much to do!"

"If we don't sleep, my love, then we won't have the energy to do all the things."

"Yeah, yeah, yeah," she said, already halfway out the door. "Hurry up and get ready. I'm gonna check on them on the way downstairs. You've got five minutes, let's go!" She smacked me on the ass before skipping out the door.

I sighed. What the hell did I get myself into?

Turns out, our snowman-building session didn't last long. We started with good intentions, but one 'accidental' snowball turned into full-blown war. At first it was couple against couple, then me and Rose versus Erica and Sam, and eventually it turned into every woman for herself.By the time we called a truce, we were soaking wet, sore from laughing, and breathless from running through the snow like big-ass kids.

While we were outside acting a fool, the chef arrived to prepare brunch. When we finally showered and got into dry clothes, the fireplace was lit, the table was set, and the food was already laid out like a holiday feast. Scrambled eggs, cheese grits, honey butter biscuits, salmon croquettes, fresh fruit, and two kinds of mimosas. This trip was turning out to be worth every freezing minute.

"Oooh, this looks so good!" Samantha said as she walked into the kitchen and saw the spread waiting for us.

"Thank you, Chef," I called out, waving as she gathered her things.

"You're more than welcome," she replied. "Dinner is in the fridge with heating instructions. You've also got everything you requested for the rest of the meals. I'll be back on the 27th. Merry Christmas, everyone!"

"Merry Christmas!" we all echoed, smiling and waving while simultaneously piling our plates with every delicious thing she left behind.

After we finished eating, we retired back to the living room, where we sprawled out across the couches. I had my head in Erica's lap while she lazily played in my hair.

"Ugh," she groaned, rubbing her stomach. "If the chef keeps cooking like that, we're not gonna do anything on this trip but eat and sleep."

"Good," I said, eyes closed, not even pretending to be mad about it.

"Hush, woman." She bent down and kissed me softly. "Okay, okay, we can all take an hour nap, but then we're decorating the tree."

She yawned in the middle of the announcement, and before she even finished her sentence, Rose and Sam were already on their way upstairs.

"You wanna go up too, baby?" I asked, sitting up a little.

"Nope. If we get in bed, we'll sleep longer than an hour. Couch is comfy and big enough."

She grabbed one of the throw blankets and curled into me. Within minutes, we were both out.

But peace didn't last long. I was jolted awake by an elbow slamming into my stomach, hard enough to knock the wind out of me. I barely got a breath out before Erica screamed, loud and raw, like she was being attacked.

Still half-asleep and on instinct, I tried to grab her from behind to calm her, not realizing it would only make things worse. She screamed again, twisting and struggling like she was fighting for her life.

"Erica! Baby, it's me!" I let her go immediately. She tumbled off the couch, hitting the floor with a thud. That must've snapped her out of it. She looked up at me, eyes wide and clouded with confusion, face streaked with tears.

"Erica," I said softly, sliding to the edge of the couch, "you're okay." I reached for her, but she held up her hand, stopping me.

"Give me a second," she said quietly.

I froze and blinked hard, trying not to let the confusion, or the sting, show on my face. It had been a while since she'd had one of these. The first few months after the kidnapping, she would wake up screaming almost every night. There were mornings I woke up with bruises I didn't even remember getting. In a way…I guess we were both still fighting demons. Just in different ways.

She sat on the floor with her knees pulled to her chest, arms wrapped tight around her legs like she was trying to hold herself together. I looked up and caught Rose standing on the staircase. She must've heard the scream, too.

She raised an eyebrow in question.

I nodded once.

We're okay.

I think.

DECEMBER 24TH
ROSE

I jolted awake to what sounded like a scream. Sam was still sound asleep beside me, breathing steadily, so it wasn't her. For a second, I thought maybe I'd dreamed it but no, I knew that sound.

I slipped quietly out of bed, careful not to wake my sleeping beauty. Halfway down the stairs, I could feel the shift in the air, the tension that hadn't been there earlier. By the time I reached the bottom, I caught the hurt flashing across Jo's face.

She looked up, saw me standing there, and I raised an eyebrow that silently asked, y'all good?

She gave me a small nod, but the uncertainty was all over her. I didn't press. Instead, I slipped into the kitchen and put on a kettle of water for tea. A few moments later, I heard the sliding door open and shut. Jo came in quietly, shoulders heavy.

"What happened?" I asked once the silence had stretched too long.

"She had a nightmare," she said softly.

"I heard her scream."

"Sorry."

"For what? Don't apologize, bro." I shook my head. "Is she still in therapy? Are you?"

Jo hesitated. "Yeah…I still go. Not weekly anymore usually once a month unless I need to… um…" Her voice cracked before she could finish.

I looked up to find her eyes glossy. "Jo," I said gently, "it's gonna be okay."

"I thought it was okay," she whispered. "She hasn't had an episode like that in months. Maybe the trip was too much. I just wanted to give her some peace after everything that happened."

"Trauma comes in waves, friend. One minute I'm fine, and the next I'm crying for no reason. I've seen all kinds of things in my line of work, but when it's personal, when it's someone you love, it hits different. Don't blame yourself or the trip. Healing's a journey, not a destination. We'll get through it together."

"Thanks, bro."

"Anytime."

"You think you could talk to her?" Jo asked. hopeful. "She's never pulled away from me like that before. She said she needed a minute, but maybe you can reach her differently. You two…went through something I didn't. You'd understand."

"I do. And yeah, I'll check on her. I made enough tea for everyone."

"Thanks," Jo murmured, managing a small smile.

I squeezed her shoulder as I passed. "Maybe check on your sister. See if she plans on waking up before lunchtime."

Jo chuckled quietly. "I'll leave that to you."

I found Erica outside by the fire pit, wrapped in one of the fur blankets.

"I thought you could use this," I said, handing her the cup of tea.

"Thanks," she whispered, wrapping her hands around the mug.

We sat in silence for a few minutes, watching the snow fall and listening to the crackle of the fire.

"I still see her sometimes," Erica said quietly. "When I close my eyes. Lying there, lifeless, blood everywhere. And she's smiling."

I looked down for a moment, then said softly, "Me too."

Her head snapped toward me. "Really?"

I nodded. "I don't get the nightmares like before, but yeah. That image… it still haunts me."

She swallowed hard. "What do you do? How do I make it stop?"

"I don't know," I admitted. "I take a deep breath. Remind myself that I'm safe, that we're safe and that she can't hurt us anymore. I forgive myself for grieving her—not because I still had feelings, but because she was human. She was hurting. I also forgive myself for not protecting Sam…and you. I go to therapy. I work out, meditate, and journal. Whatever it takes to keep healing, even when it looks different every day."

Erica nodded, taking a slow sip of tea. "Sometimes I feel like I'm going crazy, and I have to remind myself it's over."

"I get that," I said. "If Sam runs late and doesn't call, I panic. The other night when y'all were working late, she didn't answer her phone, and I almost had a full-on breakdown. If I hadn't talked to Jo, who told me where you were, I was about to get in the car and go find her."

Erica's eyes widened. "Wow. I'm sorry, Rose. I thought I was the only one still feeling the aftermath."

"We all are," I said quietly. "You think Jo and I planned this trip just for fun? Nah. We needed it, too. A chance to breathe, to forget… even if just for a little while."

"I didn't realize how much all of us are still struggling," she murmured.

I smiled faintly. "I've got an idea— something I think we should all do together. Let's go inside so I can share it with everyone."

"Yeah," she said, standing with me. "Let's do that."

We started toward the house, but she stopped me. "Rose?"

I turned. "Yeah?"

"Thank you. Not just for today, but for...that day, too."

I pulled her into a hug. "You're welcome."

DECEMBER 24TH
SAMANTHA

Damn, how long did I sleep? Erica better not have started the tree without me, I mumbled, rubbing the sleep from my eyes. I glanced at the empty bed. "Babe? You in the bathroom?"

Silence.

I pulled on some sweatpants and a long-sleeved tee, then padded downstairs. It was too quiet. Where the hell was everybody? I found Jo in the kitchen, sitting at the table with her back to me. Even from behind, I could tell something was off. Her shoulders were hunched, her head in her hands, radiating tension.

"Josie?" I asked, walking up slowly. "What's wrong?"

She flinched at my voice, startled. "Nothing. Just sitting here."

I raised an eyebrow. "So you're just sitting here... alone...looking like somebody died?"

Jo sighed, heavy. "How have you been?"

I blinked. "What do you mean, how have I been?"

"Look, I know we talk," she said, meeting my gaze. "But how have you really been?"

Something about the look in her eyes, haunted, exhausted, cut through my sarcasm. I exhaled. "I'm....okay. I guess."

Now she was the one giving me the eyebrow.

"Okay, fine. I'm better. But I still have my moments. Therapy's been helping.

I've been going every week, I don't want to go back on meds, so I'm trying to stay ahead of it. And Rose....her strength keeps me grounded. I don't know what I'd do without her. How about you?"

"Same," Jo admitted. "Better, but....I still have moments too. I cut therapy down to once a month though. I started feeling guilty going every week."

"Guilty? Why?"

She shrugged. "You and Erica were the ones who were kidnapped. Rose and Erica saw someone commit suicide. Me? I didn't go through any of that. Felt like I didn't deserve to take up space in the healing room."

I stared at her. "Jo, are you serious? You might not have been physically kidnapped, but that doesn't mean you didn't experience trauma. Your girlfriend and your twin sister were taken! You went through that fear. You put in work. You helped save us. You found Darrin shot. Don't compare trauma like it's a contest. That's not how this works."

She looked away, swallowing hard. "When you say it like that..."

"Did you tell your therapist this?"

"No. I told her I was doing better and didn't need to come as often." Her voice cracked. "But real talk, twin? This shit hit me hard. The thought of almost losing y'all... Erica's nightmares... it's a lot."

Tears slid down her face. I reached across the table and grabbed her hand. "You don't always have to be strong for us. You know that, right? You don't have to carry it all on your own."

"I just... don't want y'all to think you can't lean on me."

"We do lean on you, Jo. But you've got to let us be there for you too."

She didn't answer. Just more silent tears. I got up and moved around the table, pulling her into a hug. For once, she let me comfort her, resting her head on my shoulder like I'd done with her so many times before.

"I got you, sis."

She nodded, still silent.

"Did something happen to stir all this up? Where's Erica and Rose?"

Jo sniffed. "Erica had a nightmare. First one in months. Her scream woke Rose up. They're outside talking now."

I sat up straighter. "Damn. Why didn't you wake me up?"

She didn't respond, didn't need to. I sighed. "Well, I'm here now. And I'll keep showing up but you gotta let me in, Jo."

"I know," she whispered. "I'll do better. I'll start going to therapy more often again."

"Good. And I'll do better about checking in on you, too."

We sat quietly, rocking side to side like we used to as kids. A few minutes later, we heard the sliding door open and close. I looked up to see Rose and Erica step inside.

Jo didn't move, didn't wipe away the tear streaks or hide her vulnerability. For once, she just stayed in it. Erica sat across from us and reached for Jo's hand. Without hesitation, Jo pulled her into her lap. They wrapped themselves around each other, foreheads touching, holding on. Rose kissed me on the forehead and stood behind me, her hand resting on my shoulder. I reached up and held it.

After a moment, she cleared her throat. "I have an activity I want us to do together."

Jo and Erica looked up.

"I want us to write letters of forgiveness to ourselves. Just for your eyes to see, no one else. After we finish, we'll burn them in the fire pit. Let go of the guilt and blame we've been carrying. It won't erase what we've been through but it's a step toward healing. Y'all down?"

"I'm in," I said immediately, squeezing her hand. "That's a great idea, babe."

"Well, I can't take the credit. My therapist suggested it."

"I'm down," Jo said softly, brushing Erica's curls out of her face.

"Me too," Erica added.

"Good. I've got some paper upstairs. Be right back."

About an hour later, we were gathered around the fire pit, bundled up in blankets, letters in hand. Some of us had written more than others.

"I'll go first," I offered, standing. "I forgive myself for being set up. I didn't know, and I can't keep punishing myself for that." I dropped my letter into the flames. Jo and Rose squeezed my hands before I sat down.

"I'll go," Rose said, her voice steady. "I forgive myself for Gloria. For her coming into our lives looking for me, for not seeing what she was capable of, for not being able to save her. And for Bran." She looked at Jo as her voice cracked. Jo gave her a quiet, tearful nod. Rose tossed her letter into the fire, then sat beside me. I wrapped my arm around her waist.

Jo stood next, glancing at Erica. "I forgive myself for not knowing something I couldn't have known. For being scared. For not being able to protect the women I love. For not getting there fast enough. And for thinking I must be strong all the time." She stared into the fire, then dropped her letter in and sat down. Erica kissed her cheek.

"Well...I guess that leaves me." Erica exhaled, her voice shaky. "I forgive myself for letting Sadie in. For thinking I needed her to keep our relationship fresh. For believing I wasn't enough. And....I forgive myself because everything that happened was my fault." She tossed her letter into the fire and slumped in her seat.

"Whoa—"

"Erica—"

"Wait—"

We all started at once.

"Erica," Rose said gently, "how could this be your fault? Gloria orchestrated everything."

"If I hadn't let Sadie in, she wouldn't have had access to us."

"Or she would've found another way," Jo added.

"Best friend," I said, "you're forgetting it was me who fell for that fake bassinet setup. If you're blaming yourself, then I should too."

"None of us are to blame," Rose said firmly. "We can't carry the weight of other people's choices."

"Exactly," Jo said. "This exercise was about releasing blame, especially the blame we put on ourselves. If it's okay with y'all, I want to take it a step further."

Rose nodded.

Jo stood again. "Erica, you've always been enough. I don't blame you for Sadie. Sam, I don't blame you for being tricked. Rose, I don't blame you for Bran. You did what you thought was right. You were doing your job."

We went around, one by one, telling each other the things we needed to hear. The things we didn't even know we were still holding. I can't speak for anyone else, but that was the healing I didn't know I needed.

Afterward, we sat in silence, wrapped in each other's warmth, the fire crackling between us.

"Okay, I hate to break up the group therapy," I said finally, "but I'm starving. And it's Christmas Eve; we haven't even decorated the tree yet."

"I'm ready," Erica said, standing and stretching. She winked at Jo and reached for my hand.

As we walked back to the house, arms linked, I glanced over my shoulder and smiled. Jo and Rose were hugging, holding on just a little longer.

DECEMBER 24TH
ERICA

Back inside, I turned on the oven and pulled dinner out of the fridge. Thank God we didn't have to cook tonight. Jo really did think of everything. A few minutes later, soft R&B Christmas music started spilling through the house. The kind of playlist that makes your shoulders relax. I smiled and shook off the last of the icky weight from earlier.

Jo walked in and swept me up into one of those big bear hugs that made everything feel alright again. Then came the kiss, passionate but soft, like she needed to remind me I was safe, and loved, and hers.

"What was that for?" I asked her once she let me breathe again.

"Just because," she said, that little twinkle in her eye back where it belonged. "Why don't you go help Sam with the tree? I'll throw the lasagna in the oven and bring out some eggnog for everybody."

"Okay," I said, stroking her cheek before heading out. "I love you, Josephine Nicole."

"Ooh, not the full government," she chuckled. "I love you more, Erica Renee." She dipped back down and brushed a feather light kiss across my lips.

I floated into the living room on that kiss, only to find Sam and Rose slow dancing to Let it Snow by Boyz II Men.

"I thought we were decorating the tree?" I teased.

"I'm ready!" Sam grinned, completely unbothered.

"Sure, pal." I giggled and watched Rose give her one last dramatic twirl before disappearing upstairs.

Sam and I got to work on the huge-ass tree, finding our rhythm quickly as we strung lights, wrapped ribbon, and started hanging ornaments. Between the music, our off-key singing, and spontaneous dance breaks, we were too caught up in the moment to notice Jo watching from the kitchen.

"Dinner's ready," she called, sipping a glass of eggnog.

"What happened to bringing us a glass?" I playfully snatched hers and took a long drink.

"You two looked like you were having too much fun," she smirked. "Didn't want to disturb y'all."

Sam did a quick shoulder shimmy and danced her way into the kitchen. "It smells like the chef outdid herself again!"

We followed behind just as Rose was pulling garlic bread from the oven and slid it next to a big bowl of tossed salad.

Dinner was delicious! Cheesy, savory, warm, comforting. We stuffed ourselves like we didn't have leftovers for days and finally waddled back to the living room.

"The tree looks beautiful!" Rose said, taking a step back to admire it.

"Thanks!" I beamed. "We were gonna add a few more ornaments, but I think it looks good as is. What you think, bestie?"

Sam nodded, still chewing the last of her bread. "I think it's perfect."

"So… what's the plan?" Jo asked, sitting on the edge of the couch. "I know y'all are gonna want to fall asleep to a Christmas movie, but we should probably clean the kitchen first so we're not cooking breakfast in chaos tomorrow. What y'all think?"

"Ugh, don't remind me about breakfast. I'm gonna miss my mama's French toast casserole," I pouted.

"No, you're not. She sent me the recipe, and we've got everything we need to make it." Jo said it so casually I almost missed what she said.

"Wait, really?!" I squealed, jumping to my feet. "Woman, I love you!"

"I know," she smiled. "Why don't you and I clean the kitchen, and you can show me how to make this famous casserole?"

"Yes, yes, yes!"

"I'm sure we can find something to do," Sam winked at Rose. "What time are we meeting back here?"

I glanced at my watch. "How about nine? That gives us, like, an hour and a half?"

"Sounds good to me," Rose said, already holding Sam's hand and leading her toward the stairs.

Once in the kitchen, Jo insisted on cleaning up from dinner herself. I didn't argue, just sat at the island, sipping my eggnog and watching her move around like she owned the place.

"I still can't believe my mama really gave you that recipe," I said, grinning.

"You know your mama loves me," Jo replied with a smug little shrug.

"I know. But still. I'm excited to share this tradition with you."

"Me too, my love." She turned and offered her hand. "Now come show me how it's done."

DECEMBER 25TH
SAMANTHA

I stretched slowly, my body still heavy from all the food and emotions of the night before. The soft sheets, the warmth of the bed, and the lingering scent of peppermint and cinnamon from candles we forgot to blow out wrapped around me like a hug.

Rolling over, I smiled when I saw Rose lying next to me. For once, I was up before her. She was sleeping so peaceful, mouth slightly open. I kissed her lips gently and ran my fingers along her cheek. She stirred, then slipped her arm around my waist, pulling me close.

"Merry Christmas, baby," I whispered against her lips.

"Merry Christmas, my luv," she murmured, her voice still thick with sleep. "You're up early."

"How do you know it's early?" I raised an eyebrow.

She chuckled. "Babe, if you're awake before me, it's definitely early. Plus, it's your favorite holiday, so I figured you'd be up at the crack of dawn. What time is it?"

I glanced over my shoulder at the clock. "A little after seven."

"Oh," she stretched, "I actually slept in a little. It's not as early as I thought."

"This is sleeping in for you? On vacation?" I giggled.

"Hush, woman. You ready to get up?"

"Not yet," I said, easing her onto her back and sliding on top, straddling her with a grin.

"Mmm," she smiled, her hands already finding their way to my backside.

I lowered my head, pressing soft kisses to her neck, just beneath her ear. She squirmed, just like I knew she would. I kept going, licking and kissing the spot where her neck met her shoulder, her sweet spot, until she groaned, slid me off her, and stood up. She tugged off her boxers and let them drop to the floor. Crawling back onto the bed, she hovered above me and kissed me slow, deep, and warm.

"Top or bottom?" she whispered, brushing her lips across the top of my breasts spilling from my nightgown.

"You already know," I smirked, and she rolled over, pulling me with her until I was straddling her again.

I rolled my hips in a slow, steady rhythm while her hands roamed from my waist to my breasts, my neck and up into my hair. She pulled me down for more soft kisses as I kept moving, matching the pace of our breath.

"You feel so damn good," she murmured into the crook of my neck.

"Can we have a little extra?"

She didn't answer with words just reached into the nightstand, pulled out a bullet, turned it on, and slid it between us.

"Shit," we both gasped at the same time.

Her fingers gripped my hips while I rocked and rolled us straight into bliss. I reached my peak first, riding it out against her. I didn't stop though and a few minutes later, she stilled me on top of her, eyes closed, head tossed back as her own release washed over her.

I smiled, breathless, and bent down to kiss her. "Merry Christmas."

"Merry Christmas indeed," she whispered, pressing a kiss to my shoulder. "Let's go shower. I think I smell breakfast."

I tilted my head. "Hmmm, you're right. I smell cinnamon. They must've made the French toast casserole."

Dressed in our matching Christmas pajamas we headed downstairs. The house glowed with twinkling lights, wrapped around the banister, framing the doorways, and illuminating the crown jewel of the room, our tree. It looked like it came straight out of a movie.

Laughter and soft Christmas music floated from the kitchen. When we turned the corner, we found Jo and Erica in their own set of matching PJs in an embrace.

I cleared my throat gently, not wanting to break the vibe. "Merry Christmas!"

They turned toward us, still grinning. "Merry Christmas!" they echoed in unison.

We stepped into the kitchen, exchanging warm hugs with them both.

"It smells incredible in here," Rose said, breathing in deep.

"Thank you!" Erica beamed. "I still can't believe my mom gave Jo her secret recipe for the French toast casserole, but I'm so glad she did. It should be ready in about thirty minutes." She glanced at the oven timer with a look of pride.

"Wanna do gifts while we wait?" Jo asked.

Immediately, everyone turned to look at me.

"Why is everyone staring at me?!"

"Because we all know how you are about waiting to open gifts," Jo teased.

"I am not, okay, maybe a little." I grinned. "Fine. Let's do gifts now."

"Anyone want a mimosa?" Jo asked as she moved toward the fridge.

"Duh," Erica replied without missing a beat.

Jo laughed. "Right, my bad. Forgot who I was talking to."

"I'm gonna grab my gifts," I announced.

"Me too!" Erica grinned and we both took off toward the stairs. We met in the hallway, arms full of wrapped boxes and gift bags.

Back downstairs, Jo and Rose were already seated in the living room, each holding two mimosas. We added our gifts to the growing pile beneath the tree. Erica took a step back to snap a picture of the scene.

A few moments later, wrapping paper flew across the living room like confetti. Gift bags were scattered everywhere, and at one point, I'm pretty sure someone got bopped in the head with a flying bow. There were laughs and a few teary-eyed smiles, but mostly big, loud, heartfelt love.

Erica screamed when she opened whatever Jo got her, then immediately kissed her like she'd just proposed, again. Rose and Jo both loved the custom-designed sneakers I had made for them, and the matching Alex and Ani best friend bracelets I got for me and Erica were a hit, too.

Oh, and the engagement ring Erica gave Jo? Iconic. "People should know you're engaged, too," she said cheesing. We all laughed, but Jo was clearly ecstatic.

My favorite gift? The promise ring from Rose. Some people might think it's corny, but I loved it. We both knew we weren't ready for the marriage step just yet, but we also knew we'd get there. This ring was a quiet, beautiful declaration of our love and of our future.

Honestly, I don't even remember what I got after that. It didn't matter. This moment with us, here, together, happy, was the best gift I could've asked for.

The oven timer dinged and Jo stood up to grab the casserole.

"I'll help you, sis." I followed behind her.

"We'll clean up all this gift wrap," Erica offered as she and Rose began gathering the scraps.

"NO!" Jo and I both turned around in unison.

They froze, mid-bend, confusion written all over their faces.

Jo spoke first, gently grabbing my hand. "When we were little and our parents were still here, they insisted we leave the mess and just enjoy the day. It made the room feel more—"

"Lived in and festive," I finished for her. "Our dad used to say, Christmas and home aren't about looking perfect. It's about who you share it with. So, we leave the mess and soak in the moment."

"It's something we've tried to live by ever since," Jo added softly.

"I love that," Erica said, her voice tender.

"Then let's leave the mess!" Rose laughed, tossing the wrapping paper she was holding into the air like confetti.

Jo and I exchanged a smile before turning back toward the kitchen. She wrapped her arm around my shoulder as we walked.

❄ ❄ ❄

"I have eaten way too much. I feel like a stuffed pig," Erica groaned, leaning back in her chair.

"Same," I said with a full-belly smile, rubbing my stomach. "That casserole is officially my new favorite food."

"I'm not too full for another mimosa," Rose said, already reaching to refill her glass from the pitcher Jo made.

"Me either," Jo added, handing over her glass.

Erica and I got up to clear the table, scraping off the plates and tossing the trash. Once everything was cleaned, we all headed back to the living room. I smiled at the beautiful chaos of wrapping paper still scattered across the floor. It felt right.

Each couple cozied up on their own couch, curled under fur blankets. Rose put on a Christmas movie, but I had a feeling the movie would end up watching us instead of the other way around.

JANUARY 2ND
ROSE

"I don't want to go home," Sam pouted as she tossed her toiletry bag into her suitcase and zipped it shut. She'd said that at least three times already this morning and had moved slower than molasses getting dressed. Jo and I had planned for this, though. We told her and Erica the car was picking us up an hour earlier than it actually was.

"I know," I said, taking both her hands in mine and kissing them. "At least we still have a few days off before work starts back up. We can keep the vacation going when we get home."

"But there's no snow at home," she huffed.

"I figured you'd be over snow after you flew off your snowmobile like an Olympic gymnast," I teased.

"That's not funny! I saw my life flash before my eyes." She tried to pout, but we both broke into uncontrollable laughter, holding our stomachs.

"I'm still not sure how you even managed that."

"Shit, me either!" She wheezed, wiping tears from her face.

"Come on. We've got time for one last cocoa in front of the fireplace," I grabbed her suitcase with one hand and her hand with the other, leaving our room behind. We followed the sound of Jo and Erica's laughter into the kitchen.

"What's so funny?" Sam asked, filling two mugs from the warm pot of Erica's special cocoa.

"You wiping out on the snowmobile," Jo cackled, nearly spilling her own drink.

Sam rolled her eyes but laughed anyway. "Okay, yeah… it was kinda funny."

We took our cocoa into the living room and settled near the fireplace, the lights on the tree still twinkling softly.

"I don't know what's been better, the peace and quiet or the food," Erica sighed.

"The food has been top tier," I said, raising my mug. "Jo, send me the chef's info. I want to give her an extra tip."

"No doubt," Jo nodded. "But I think my favorite part was all the snow fun, the snowball fights, snow angels and even our snowman contest. I haven't laughed that hard in forever."

"That were definitely a highlight," Sam added. "Me and Erica's snowman actually turned out cute once we figured out what we were doing."

"Not to sound corny, but honestly? My favorite part was just being here. With y'all. No drama, no distractions. Just us." I pulled Sam in closer beside me. "And Erica, we owe your parents a thank you for that cruise. If they hadn't gone, this wouldn't have happened."

"Right?" Jo grinned. "Bless them for canceling Christmas on you."

"Not canceling Christmas!" Erica laughed. "But I'll admit, this turned out better than anything I could've planned. This time together? It was everything I needed."

"Maybe we turn this into a tradition," Sam said. "Even if it's not Christmas, we could come back every year, afterwards. A post-holiday getaway."

"I love that." I looked at Jo and Erica for their vote.

They exchanged a quick glance.

"Speaking of a getaway – " Jo started.

"We're having a destination wedding!" Erica blurted, eyes gleaming.

"For real?!" Sam squealed.

"Yup! So now we've got two vacations to plan, one to relax and one for my wedding!" Erica practically bounced out of her seat, dragging Sam with her into the kitchen as they started discussing wedding plans.

I looked over at Jo, who was grinning like a kid with a secret.

"So… have y'all picked a date and place?"

Jo's smile widened. "Yeah, we have."

O'Jay Barr is a native of Trenton, NJ, currently living in Atlanta, GA. She writes lesbian romance and drama, with plans to branch into other genres, true to her brand tagline: Repping the Rainbow One Genre at a Time. This holiday short features characters from her trilogy series The Other Side. Be sure to follow her on all social media @ AUTHOR_OJAYBARR